SILLY MILLY ADVENTURES
SILLY MILLY
and the Picture Day Sillies

Written by
Laurie Friedman

Illustrated by
Lauren Rodriguez

A Blossoms Beginning Readers Book

CRABTREE
Publishing Company
www.crabtreebooks.com

BLOSSOMS BEGINNING READERS LEVEL GUIDE

Level 1 Early Emergent Readers Grades PK-K
Books at this level have strong picture support with carefully controlled text and repetitive patterns. They feature a limited number of words on each page and large, easy-to-read print.

Level 2 Emergent Readers Grade 1
Books at this level have a more complex sentence structure and more lines of text per page. They depend less on repetitive patterns and pictures. Familiar topics are explored, but with greater depth.

Level 3 Early Readers Grade 2
Books at this level are carefully developed to tell a great story, but in a format that children are able to read and enjoy by themselves. They feature familiar vocabulary and appealing illustrations.

Level 4 Fluent Readers Grade 3
Books at this level have more text and use challenging vocabulary. They explore less familiar topics and continue to help refine and strengthen reading skills to get ready for chapter books.

School-to-Home Support for Caregivers and Teachers

This book helps children grow by letting them practice reading. Here are a few guiding questions to help the reader with building his or her comprehension skills. Possible answers appear here in red.

Before Reading:
- What do I think this story will be about?
  - *I think this story will be about a girl named Milly who likes to act silly.*
  - *I think this story will be about picture day.*

During Reading:
- Pause and look at the words and pictures. Why did the character do that?
  - *I think Milly is being silly on picture day because she likes to make Jack laugh.*
  - *I think Milly's mom does not like her being silly today because she wants the picture to look nice.*

After Reading:
- Describe your favorite part of the story.
  - *My favorite part was when Milly and Jack were having fun being silly together.*
  - *I liked the part when Milly and her family were silly together.*

Milly likes to be silly.

Milly likes to be silly with Jack.
Jack is a baby.
Jack is Milly's baby brother.

Today is picture day.
Mom is taking Milly and Jack
to have their picture taken.

Milly smiles very silly.
Milly says, "Cheese."
Jack claps. Jack laughs.

"Cheese," says Milly.
"Cheese. Cheese. Cheese."

"Today is picture day," says Mom.

"Today is NOT a good day to be silly," says Mom.

But Milly likes to be silly.
Jack likes when Milly is silly.

"Are you ready?" asks Mom.
Milly is ready.

Milly is ready to have her picture taken.
Milly meets the man who will take her picture.
His name is Ted.

Ted tells Milly to sit in a chair.
Jack sits next to Milly.

Ted counts to three.
"Say cheese," says Ted.

Milly smiles very silly. Milly says, "Cheese."
Jack laughs. Jack claps.

"Cheese," says Milly. "Cheese. Cheese. Cheese."
Jack likes when Milly is silly.

But Mom does not like it. Not today. "Today is NOT a good day to be silly," says Mom.

Milly and Jack sit in the chair.
Ted counts to three.
"Say cheese," says Ted.

Milly does not even say cheese.
But Jack claps.
Jack laughs.
Milly claps.
Milly laughs too.

Milly and Jack have the sillies.
Milly is happy.
Jack is happy.

Mom is not happy.
Ted is not happy.

Mom tells Milly and Jack to sit in the chair.
"NO more sillies!" says Mom.

"Today is picture day," says Mom. "Today is NOT a good day to be silly."

Mom looks at Milly.
"Milly," says Mom.
"You are the big sister.
It is up to you to show
Jack what to do."

"Do you understand?" asks Mom.
Milly understands.

Milly sits in the chair.
Jack sits in the chair
"No more sillies,"
Milly tells Jack.

Ted counts to three.
"Smile," says Ted.
Milly smiles.
Jack smiles.
Ted takes the picture.

Ted shows the picture to Mom.
Mom smiles. Ted smiles.

Mom is proud of Milly.
Mom is proud of Jack.

Sometimes it is NOT a good time to be silly.

But sometimes it is. Sometimes it is a very good time to be silly.

ABOUT THE AUTHOR

Laurie Friedman is the award-winning author of more than seventy-five critically acclaimed picture books, chapter books, and novels for young readers, including the bestselling *Mallory McDonald* series and the *Love, Ruby Valentine* series. She is a native Arkansan, and in addition to writing, loves to read, bake, do yoga, and spend time with her friends and family. For more information about Laurie and her books, please visit her website at www.lauriebfriedman.com.

ABOUT THE ILLUSTRATOR

Lauren Rodriguez is an illustrator and character designer in the LA area. She loves passion fruit tea, nighttime, paranormal podcasts, and her two doggies (Annie and Teddy).

Written by: Laurie Friedman
Illustrations by: Lauren Rodriguez
Art direction and layout by: Rhea Wallace

Series Development: James Earley
Proofreader: Kathy Middleton
Educational Consultant: Marie Lemke M.Ed.
Print and production coordinator:
Katherine Berti

Library and Archives Canada Cataloguing in Publication

Title: Silly Milly and the picture day sillies / written by Laurie Friedman ; illustrated by Lauren Rodriguez.
Names: Friedman, Laurie B., 1964- author. | Rodriguez, Lauren (Illustrator), illustrator.
Description: Series statement: Silly Milly adventures | "A blossoms beginning readers book".
Identifiers: Canadiana (print) 2021023668X |
    Canadiana (ebook) 20210236698 |
    ISBN 9781427152688 (hardcover) |
    ISBN 9781427152749 (softcover) |
    ISBN 9781427152800 (HTML) |
    ISBN 9781427152862 (EPUB) |
    ISBN 9781427152923 (read-along ebook)
Classification: LCC PZ7.F7493 Sip 2022 | DDC j813/.6—dc23

Library of Congress Cataloging-in-Publication Data

Names: Friedman, Laurie B., 1964- author. | Rodriguez, Lauren (Illustrator), illustrator.
Title: Silly Milly and the picture day sillies / written by Laurie Friedman ; illustrated by Lauren Rodriguez.
Description: New York, NY : Crabtree Publishing Company, [2022] | Series: Silly Milly Adventures - A Blossoms Beginning Readers Book
Identifiers: LCCN 2021027024 (print) |
    LCCN 2021027025 (ebook) |
    ISBN 9781427152688 (hardcover) |
    ISBN 9781427152749 (paperback) |
    ISBN 9781427152800 (ebook) |
    ISBN 9781427152862 (epub) |
    ISBN 9781427152923
Subjects: LCSH: Readers (Primary) | LCGFT: Readers (Publications) | Picture books.
Classification: LCC PE1119.2 .F7586 2022 (print) | LCC PE1119.2 (ebook) | DDC 428.6/2--dc23
LC record available at https://lccn.loc.gov/2021027024
LC ebook record available at https://lccn.loc.gov/2021027025

Crabtree Publishing Company

www.crabtreebooks.com   1-800-387-7650

Copyright © 2022 **CRABTREE PUBLISHING COMPANY**

All rights reserved. No part of this publication may be reproduced, stored in a retrieval system or be transmitted in any form or by any means, electronic, mechanical, photocopying, recording, or otherwise, without the prior written permission of Crabtree Publishing Company. In Canada: We acknowledge the financial support of the Government of Canada through the Canada Book Fund for our publishing activities.

Published in the United States
Crabtree Publishing
347 Fifth Avenue, Suite 1402-145
New York, NY, 10016

Published in Canada
Crabtree Publishing
616 Welland Ave.
St. Catharines, ON, L2M 5V6

Printed in the U.S.A./072021/CG20210514